PROTECTING HIS CURVY GIRL

SUNSET SECURITY BOOK TWO

SADIE KING

PROTECTING HIS CURVY GIRL

SUNSET SECURITY BOOK TWO

How far would you go to feed your obsession?

When a client shows me Kayla's photo, I'm intrigued by the carefree blonde with the wide smile.

Her father is worried some creep will violate his little girl, and he employs me to keep watch over her.

He doesn't realize he's feeding my obsession, or how far I'll go to get Kayla in my life.

Now we're playing happy families, me and Kayla, shacked up and falling in love.

But she doesn't know what I've done, that I'm the creep. I'm the man her Daddy warned her about.

Protecting His Curvy Girl is a sweet-stalker, age-gap romance featuring an OTT obsessive ex-military man and a curvy woman he'll do anything to make his own.

DON'T MISS OUT!

Want to be the first to hear about new releases and special offers?
Follow Sadie King on BookBub to get an alert whenever she has a new release, preorder, or discount!

www.bookbub.com/authors/sadie-king

CONTENTS

1. Seth — 1
2. Kayla — 6
3. Seth — 10
4. Kayla — 16
5. Seth — 21
6. Kayla — 26
7. Seth — 28
8. Kayla — 33
9. Seth — 38
10. Kayla — 41
11. Seth — 45
12. Kayla — 49
13. Seth — 54
14. Kayla — 57
15. Kayla — 61
16. Seth — 65
17. Kayla — 70
18. Seth — 72
19. Kayla — 76
    Epilogue — 82

What to read next — 85
His Nightly Obsession — 87
Get your FREE Book — 89
Books by Sadie King — 91
About the Author — 93

1
SETH

The man rests half an ass cheek on my desk and folds his arms across his chest.

My left hand twitches, and I drum my fingers on my thigh. I hate people touching my desk. But I'm good mannered enough not to say anything.

The man is a guest in my home. Well, kind of.

Patrick Folley is a potential client, and Bronn asked to do the meeting at my home office because it's the kind of job that requires my particular set of special skills.

Although, judging by the incredulous look on Bronn's face, I'm not sure we're going to take the job.

"You want us to spy on your daughter?" Bronn repeats what Patrick has just told us, though Patrick went about it in a more roundabout kind of way. "We're a security firm. We provide security. We're not private detectives."

"I know what you are," Patrick says, unfolding his arms and fixing Bronn with a steely stare. "You're ex-special forces. We all know that means James Bond kind of shit."

I sigh inwardly and keep my gaze well away from Bronn, or else we'd both end up rolling our eyes.

"Not quite," Bronn chuckles.

He's much better at client relations than I am. I'd have told this guy to fuck off.

"It means we're tough motherfuckers who aren't afraid of a fight. You want security on your girl, we've got her covered. But we don't do spying."

Patrick holds up his hands. There are calluses on his palms and a plain gold band squeezed on his thick finger that looks like it hasn't come off in years. I wonder how he made his money because he does have money. Otherwise, he wouldn't be here.

"You misunderstand me. I don't want to know what my daughter is doing." He winces slightly. He does care what she's doing. He cares very much. "She wants her freedom, and I'm not going to get in her way. But it's a big scary world out there, and if something were to happen to her…"

He trails off and puts a hand over his eyes. The gesture is so sincere that I feel sorry for the guy. This is more than a regular father looking out for his daughter. I'd bet a week of beer money that there's more to this story than a protective father not wanting his little girl to grow up.

My fingers itch to get on my keyboard and look into this guy. I flex them and clasp my hands together.

I'll have to wait 'til he leaves before I do any digging. Even if we don't take the job, and I can tell from the look on Bronn's face that it's unlikely, my curiosity has been piqued.

It's an occupational hazard in my line of work—

curiosity. Having to know everything about everyone makes me good at what I do.

Patrick lowers his hand and gives Bronn a weak smile.

"I just want you to keep an eye on her. Watch where she's going and who she's hanging out with. If she's out at night, make sure she gets home safe. If she meets anyone online, make sure they're not an asshole."

I glance at Bronn. This is why I'm here. If you want online surveillance, I'm your guy. But it's a gray area, legally and ethically.

"I don't need to know who she's spending time with. I just need to know she's all right. And if there's ever any danger, if she's in any trouble, you step in."

"You want twenty-four-hour surveillance on your daughter?" Bronn asks.

There's uncertainty in his voice, and I don't blame him. Babysitting isn't our usual gig.

"Yes," Patrick says simply. "That's what I want."

Bronn looks at me. I meet his gaze and shake my head almost imperceptibly, letting him know I don't think it's a good idea.

We're a security firm. Any surveillance we do usually has the consent of the person we're watching. It feels too sneaky for me, invading a young woman's privacy just to give her old man peace of mind.

"I can pay you double your usual fee," Patrick adds hastily.

This makes Bronn pause. Not because he needs the money, but because this guy must be desperate.

Patrick takes his butt off my desk and pulls a wad of

cash out of his pocket. "Here's the first payment right here."

It's a lot of money, and he shoves it at Bronn, a look of desperation on his face.

Bronn doesn't take the money. He shakes his head slowly, but before he can speak, the man takes a photo out of his back pocket and holds it up to us.

"This is Kayla."

The photo shows two young women smiling widely. They both have the same sunshine-colored hair and apple-shaped cheeks. The one on the left has her hair cut short in a severe cut, her eye makeup drawn dramatically. But it's the one on the right I can't take my eyes off.

Her hair falls in soft waves over her shoulders. Her arm's dropped casually around the woman who must be her sister, and her head's tilted back in a laugh, showing straight white teeth and a pink tongue. She's not wearing any makeup, but her looks are striking. Pale skin and full lips, a dusting of freckles over her cherub nose.

"Which one's Kayla?"

It's the first time I've spoken, and Patrick looks at me in surprise, like he's forgotten I'm here. I'm used to that reaction. I'm good at blending into the background, at going unnoticed.

"The one on the right." He taps the photo, indicating the laughing girl with sparkling eyes and full lips.

The more I stare at the photo, the stranger I feel, like I know her, like I've always known her. Even though I'm sure we've never met.

Bronn opens his mouth to say something, but I get in first.

"We'll take the job."

I can feel Bronn's eyes shooting daggers at me, but I don't look at him. I keep my eyes on that photo, on the girl who I've never met but whose image I know will forever be etched into my brain.

She's the most beautiful woman I've ever seen. Her carefree look and laughter are what I fought for.

The man is shaking my hand gratefully, telling me how thankful he is. I barely hear him I'm so focused on that picture.

"I'll need this."

I snatch the photo out of his hands and push up out of my chair.

While Patrick works out the details with Bronn, I head over to my main PC and bank of computer screens.

I've been sitting so long that pins and needles shoot through my bad leg. It fucking hurts when I stand up, but I keep my expression neutral.

Dragging my leg over to the desk at the far side of the room, I tuck the photo into the side of the screen and fire up the main PC.

I'm already typing "Kayla Folley" into my search engine before the man leaves. I have to know everything about this woman.

2
KAYLA

The whirl of the industrial dishwasher is strangely comforting, probably because it signals I'm almost at the end of my shift. With the last of the dishes being washed, I grab the broom, humming as I sweep the floor.

The bell above the door jingles, and I look up to see Mira waddling in the door.

Her cheeks are flushed red, and one hand holds her enormous belly.

"Shouldn't you be resting?"

I don't know much about pregnancy, but I know when you're as round as Mira is, it's almost time to get to the hospital.

She waves a hand dismissively. "I've still got another three weeks to go. How are you getting on?"

I've only been at the job for two weeks and I've already formed a connection with Mira, the owner of the Something Fishy Cafe and my new boss.

"We had a group tour in for lunch today and they ate us out of crab."

Mira nods. "Sean will drop some off when his boat gets in tomorrow morning."

Mira's husband's a local fisherman, and he keeps the cafe well supplied.

"And how are you sleeping? Not too quiet here for you?"

The accommodation upstairs came with the job. Not only is Mira my boss, she's also my landlady. She looks concerned, as if I might find Temptation Bay too dull and run off back to Portland. As if. I came for a change, for a break from the city, and Temptation Bay with its sleepy marina and one row of shops is perfect.

"It's fine. Thanks."

And it is. The two-bedroom apartment is small and basic, a world away from the plush, three-story home I grew up in, but that's why I love it. I needed to get out on my own, and this place is perfect.

Mira rubs her belly, and an uncomfortable look crosses her face.

"I'm supposed to have another three weeks, but with the way this one is kicking, I'd be surprised if he lasts that long."

She eases herself into a seat, and I grab her a glass of water.

"Do you want me to call Sean?"

Her husband is a quiet man, but the way he looks at Mira, and the way he's always got one arm on her protectively, makes me think he wouldn't be too happy that she's out and about.

She shakes her head.

"Please don't. Sean would have had me at home in bed for the last six months if he could. He's more anxious about this pregnancy than I am."

She smiles as she says it, and a warm look comes over her face. I feel a pang of yearning, wondering if I'll ever meet a man that's as fiercely protective of me as Sean is of Mira.

While Mira finishes her water, I sweep up the last of the trash and put the bins out back. Then I hang my apron up and grab my purse.

"You gonna hang around, or can I lock up?"

Mira pulls herself out of her chair. "Lock up. I'm going home before Sean comes looking for me. I just wanted to make sure you're okay with everything."

I know Mira is worried about her business and what will happen when she has the baby. I give her my most reassuring smile.

"It's all fine. I've got it under control."

She looks relieved, and I'm thankful that Dad insisted that me and my sister get part-time jobs even though he could afford to give us everything we need. My dad is a self-made man, and he values hard work. He didn't want to give us the easy life.

I got a weekend job at the local cafe when I was sixteen and was duty manager a few years later. It means I've got the experience to handle things here for Mira.

I lock up and say goodbye to Mira. She waddles off to her car, and I take a walk along the waterfront.

"There you are, Mr. Red."

A seagull watches me from his perch on one of the

wooden bollards. I take the bag of bread crusts out of my purse and throw a handful to the ground.

Mr. Red regards me for a moment as if deciding whether the crumbs are worth his time, then there's the beating of wings, and he flies down to snatch up the crumbs by my feet.

He's joined by some of his friends, and they fight over the bits of bread.

"There's enough for everyone," I tell the noisy gulls.

I take a seat on a bench overlooking the water and scatter the last of the breadcrumbs for the birds.

The cawing noise blends with the gentle breaking of the waves against the shore. The late afternoon sun hits my face, and I close my eyes and tilt my head up to catch the warmth of the sun's rays.

At moments like this, I feel happy to be here. Happy to be in the fresh air, away from the city. Away from everything that happened.

My mind wanders to my father and his visit yesterday.

He worries about me, of course he does, especially after what happened to Jo. But he didn't try to take me home.

Dad understands I need to do this. I need time away from my family, time to be on my own and to find myself. He's a self-made man, so he knows the importance of independence.

I don't know how long I'll stay in Temptation Bay. I don't know if I'll move on somewhere else or if I'll go back home.

I don't have to think about that now. I just have to close my eyes and enjoy the sun. That's all I have to do.

3
SETH

Kayla Folley. Nineteen years old. Youngest daughter of Patrick Folley, who made his modest fortune with a forklift business based out of Portland.

This is a fraction of the information that I've been able to find out about the young woman I'm being paid to watch.

It was easy to find out about her family from local online groups and magazines due to her father's philanthropy in the community.

From scrolling Kayla's social feeds, I learned that she loves animals, is obsessed with an indie band called The Matching Patterns, is first-aid trained, and played hockey in school.

I also know her credit card details, her PIN number, and the password she uses for most of her online logins.

Armed with this information and using a few of my special skills, I find myself staring into Kayla's living room, my heart racing as I watch her munch on a bag of

Doritos with her feet tucked up on the couch as she watches a renovation show on the TV.

She's even more beautiful than her photograph. Her hair is pulled casually off her face, and her t-shirt clings to her curvy figure. Her breasts move every time she leans forward to scoop salsa onto her corn chip from a jar on the coffee table.

I shouldn't be here watching this private moment. I feel like an intruder—I am an intruder—but I'm unable to look away.

It's easy to hack into a camera on a device once you know how. I tried to get into Kayla's laptop, but she keeps it closed most of the time. So I've gone in through her smart TV.

Kayla doesn't know I'm here. I shouldn't be here. This is beyond what her father asked me to do. But ever since I started watching Kayla, I haven't been able to stop.

One of the screens in my bank of monitors flickers, and I pull my gaze away from the beauty on the couch.

In front of me is a wall of screens showing the feeds from various CCTV cameras around Temptation Bay.

For the last few days, I've been tracing the paths that Kayla walks, making sure she's keeping safe like her father is paying me to do.

But it's more than that. Once I started tracking Kayla, I couldn't stop.

She fascinates me, the young woman who left her wealthy family behind to come to a small beach town.

What made her give up that comfortable life for a small apartment and a job in a cafe?

I've hacked into every single security camera in Temptation Bay. There's good coverage. A few black spots, but I can mostly see the whole town from here.

Not that I'm interested. The only person I want to watch is sitting on the couch with a hand in a bag of Doritos.

It's making me hungry.

Something soft rubs against my leg, and I reach down absentmindedly to stroke Felix. He meows and jumps into my lap, making me sit back from the screens.

"You hungry too, buddy?"

Felix nuzzles into my hand, and I take that to mean yes. It's a hazardous position being a pet to someone like me. I can get so engrossed in a task that hours will pass without me realizing.

Luckily, Felix is here to remind me to get up once in a while and eat.

"Come on then."

Felix leaps off my lap as I stand up. There's a dull ache in my leg, and I walk around the room a few times until the blood's flowing again.

Felix mewls impatiently, so I limp through to the kitchen.

"All right, buddy. I'll get you something."

I open a can of tuna and dump half of it on Felix's plate and make a sandwich out of the rest. He's got to be the best-fed cat on the coast.

Felix purrs as he eats, the rumbling noise familiar and comforting. I give him a rub behind the ears before taking my sandwich to the other room.

Kayla's still on the couch where I left her. She's smiling

PROTECTING HIS CURVY GIRL

at something on the TV, her face lighting up and radiating her natural beauty.

Even in sweatpants and a baggy t-shirt she's beautiful. More than beautiful. She's radiant in a way that pulls at my heart and stirs something deep in my gut.

Something makes her laugh, and her breasts bounce up and down under the t-shirt.

My dick stirs along with my gut, and now I feel like a big old pervert, getting off on someone who doesn't know I'm watching.

But I can't look away. There's something captivating about this woman, something that makes me want to never let her out of my sight.

Reaching to my mixing desk, I turn the volume from her TV up so I can hear her laugh. It's fucking beautiful, like the rest of her.

There's a function to be able to watch a movie or game together and chat through your TV, but I make sure my sound is muted.

She can't know that I'm here.

Because I shouldn't be here.

Surveillance can be a gray area, which is why Bronn didn't want to take the job. If you want to keep an eye on someone without them knowing, then doing it virtually is the safe option.

Sure, I could tail Kayla, watch her cafe and follow her everywhere, but in a small town like this, it wouldn't be long before she noticed me.

If her father wants to ensure her safety, then this is the way to do it. Virtually. Although, even I know this is not what he had in mind.

He wants to make sure his daughter is safe when she goes out, and that if she's meeting anyone online that they're not going to harm her. He's got a good reason to be protective of her.

When I was researching Kayla, I found out about her sister, Jo.

Last year, Jo was sexually assaulted by a man she met online. Her family kept it out of the papers, but I was able to hack the police records.

I knew there must be a reason her father was overconcerned, wanting to give his daughter the freedom she needs but terrified something similar might happen.

That's why I've hacked all of Kayla's online accounts. If she meets anyone online, I'll know about it.

A surge of heat courses through my veins, and I clench my fists. If she meets anyone online, I'll shut him down.

Not because that's what her father, my client, would want, but because Kayla's mine. I know it in my gut.

Luckily, Kayla doesn't seem interested in online dating. In the two days I've been watching her, she's come home from her job at the cafe, which is downstairs from her apartment, and watched TV. Sometimes she reads. Sometimes she talks to her friends. But on the whole, my Kayla is a homebody, just like me.

I could watch Kayla all night, but I won't. It's time to give her some privacy. She's safe for the night, and that's all I need to know.

"Goodnight, sweetheart," I say, knowing she can't hear me.

With reluctance, I turn off the feed, leaving her alone to enjoy her Doritos.

The room feels empty without Kayla's image on the screen, and I miss her already.

My heart aches for this woman, this woman who I've never met, who wouldn't look twice at a wounded older man with a limp who is more comfortable around computer screens than people. Which is why I prefer to observe.

From the safety of my room, I can dream about talking with Kayla, laughing with her and sharing her life. But what would a young, radiant woman like Kayla see in a broken man like me?

4
KAYLA

As I turn the key to lock the cafe, the seagulls are already circling.

"All right, calm down," I call to Mr. Red. He flutters to the ground, pulling in his wings and looking chastised.

"I've got enough for all of you," I tell the impatient birds.

I don't want them hanging around the cafe, so I walk along the waterfront until I'm out of the way of the shops. It's not 'til I'm almost at the pier that I open my bag of breadcrumbs.

The birds flutter into the air, cawing at each other as they compete for the tidbits.

I've only got a few handfuls of bread, and it doesn't take long to throw all of it to my bird friends.

"That's all for today."

Mr. Red cocks his head, and I like to think he's nodding a thank you.

I'm shaking the crumbs out of the bag when the birds

disperse. As one, they lift into the air, cawing to each other as they fly away and come to land a little further along the waterfront. I squint into the sun, trying to see what's caught their attention.

There's a man sitting on a bench, dipping his hand into a bread bag.

A smile creeps across my face. The cheeky beggars are getting a second snack.

I glance around to check I'm not on my own walking toward a stranger, but the waterfront is busy with locals hurrying home from work and tourists out for a pre-dinner stroll.

Nevertheless, there's a pinch of anxiety in my gut. There always is after what happened to Jo.

I'm heading in that direction anyway, and I stroll toward the bench, shaking out the last of the crumbs from my bag.

When I'm nearly at the bench, the man turns around, and my breath catches in my chest. He's hot, like really hot, with rugged features and a peppering of stubble on his chiseled chin. The sun glints off his blond hair, making him look for a moment like he's got a halo.

"No matter how much you give them, they're always hungry." His voice is deep and soft, like it could lull me to sleep, which may be why the birds like him.

But I can't judge someone by the timbre of his voice. I'm uncertain whether I should get into a conversation with a strange man, but he's got a kind smile, and anyone who feeds the seagulls must be a good person.

"That one's Mr. Red," I tell him, pointing to the biggest

seagull. I immediately feel stupid. Naming seagulls like they're stuffed animals. This man's clearly older than me, and I desperately don't want him to think I'm childish.

But he just smiles and looks over at the big seagull.

"Mr. Red," he says. "It suits him."

He turns his gaze back to me, and I notice how blue his eyes are—deep blue like the ocean.

"I'm Seth."

I hesitate, not sure if I should give him my name.

I've been given the stranger-danger talk so many times in the last year that it's a wonder I ever leave the house.

Don't give anyone your real name online. Don't tell them where you live. If you're meeting someone you've met online, go somewhere public and go with a friend.

It makes sense after what happened to Jo, but it's also suffocating. My dad's become so overprotective of me that it's hard to want to go out or meet anyone at all.

It's part of the reason I had to get away. I needed some space. I know to be careful, but I still want to have a life.

I make a split-second judgement to trust this man, Seth. I mean, he feeds seagulls, and he smiles with his eyes. He can't be a creep.

"I'm Kayla."

Seth nods slowly. "Did you name him Mr. Red because of his red beak or because of his red feet?"

I look at Mr. Red, and his beady eye regards me carefully.

"It was the beak. It's so much bigger than the others. I thought he must be the leader of the flock. If flocks have leaders…"

I trail off, feeling stupid again. I know nothing about birds, and I don't know why I'm talking about birds. I just know I want to keep this man's gaze on me.

"That makes sense."

He nods thoughtfully as if what I've said is the most profound thing ever.

"I like this little cheeky one over here. He's pretending to have one leg, but as soon as you throw some bread over, bam, his other leg comes down and he snaps it up."

We watch the seagulls for a while, making comments on their character traits. Seth makes me laugh. He's funny and thoughtful and freakin' hot.

He doesn't ask me anything personal, and he doesn't ask me out, which I feel relieved and disappointed about at the same time.

Daddy lectured me about not going out with strange men, but how do they ever not become strangers if you can't get to know them? And Seth is a man I'd like to get to know.

After a while, Seth stands up and tucks the empty bread bag in his pocket.

"It was nice meeting you, Kayla."

I feel sad that he's leaving, but I don't know how to make him stay. It's too forward to ask him out, so I don't say anything.

"Nice meeting you too."

As he walks away, he drags his left leg a little as if it pains him. I want to ask him what the injury is, how he got it. I want to ask him if he'll be back tomorrow to feed the seagulls.

But anxiety gnaws in my stomach. I shouldn't talk to strange men because they might be assholes who will assault you any chance they get. But how does someone move from stranger to acquaintance if you're not supposed to talk to them?

5
SETH

She's on the couch again, eating cheesy pasta right out of the pan while watching a reality TV show about couples renovating their homes.

I can hear every word. With the volume turned up on my mixing desk, I hear both the TV and Kayla's laughter.

I've been watching her for five days, and I know all the shows she watches, all the people she speaks to.

Her father has nothing to be worried about. Kayla is enjoying her freedom by eating bad food and watching crappy television. I'm betting she didn't get to do those things in her other life.

From what I've been able to find out, her father was pushy with her education, determined his girls would have a better start to life than he did.

Kayla sets the pan on the floor and curls up with her feet tucked under her. The curve of her leg is outlined through her thin leggings, and my gaze traces the outline of her body as I think about her legs and the dark center at the top of them.

There's a stirring in my trousers, and my dick lengthens.

At that moment, Felix jumps onto my lap, his claws digging into my goods.

"Fuck!"

His sharp claws penetrate my sweatpants and dig right into my cock. I pull my legs up, and Felix jumps out of the way and onto my desk. His feet scramble on the mixing desk, and his tail swishes, knocking over my empty coffee cup.

"Shit, Felix. What are you doing, buddy?"

Kayla sits up ramrod straight on the couch, staring at the TV.

"Who said that?"

She's peering at the TV in a strange way. It's a quiet part of the program. There's just some music playing as they show a timelapse of the building.

Felix mewls, and I clutch him around the waist.

"Get down, you." I lift him off the desk, and he leaps from my arms to the floor.

"What the fuck?" Kayla says to the TV.

My stomach drops as I realize what's happening. She can hear me.

My hand darts to the mixing desk. The slider that controls my audio has been turned up, no longer on mute. Felix must have knocked it when he jumped up there.

Shit.

I hesitate with my hand hovering over the slider. Kayla looks freaked out, and I don't blame her, but this is also my opportunity to talk to her, to speak to her without her seeing it's the broken man she met on the waterfront.

"Hey," I say into the microphone.

Her eyes go wide, and she jumps up from the couch.

"Who said that?"

She looks around her apartment, and her gaze comes to rest on the TV.

I don't want to scare her any more than she is already, and I wrack my brain for something to say that isn't creepy.

"Are you enjoying the show?"

I wince at the inanity of it. But if I say anything personal, she'll freak out even more.

"How the fuck are you talking to me?"

Her hands rise in a WTF gesture. I don't know how to calm her down, to turn this around.

"I've linked into your TV."

Her mouth drops open in surprise, making her look fucking adorable.

"How the fuck did you do that?"

Kayla swears a lot when she's freaking out, which is probably a sign I should leave her alone. But this might be my only chance to talk to her.

"It's complicated."

She narrows her eyes at the TV.

"Well, you can fuck right off."

Picking up the remote, she turns the TV off. I use the opportunity to put my mic on mute. Let her think turning the TV off will solve the problem.

It doesn't. I'm still here. Still watching.

She breathes heavily, her hands on her hips, her nostrils flaring.

In another moment, she reaches behind the TV and,

I'm guessing, yanks the plug out of the wall. Sensible girl. That does cut my connection.

I have no eyes on Kayla, and I feel the loss deep in my chest.

Tapping my keyboard, I bring up the feed to her laptop. It's dead. I tap some more and bring up her phone.

She's searching "TV hacked," which will probably scare the shit out of her even more.

I don't have access to her phone camera, so I can't see her face. I can't see if she's worried or scared or upset.

I hate the thought of her being any of those things. And knowing I've caused it is even worse.

I was stupid to try to start up a conversation. If I'd muted immediately, she probably would have thought it was a network error.

Sometimes I live so long in my online world that I forget this isn't normal.

I watch the feed from her phone as she scrolls through articles about smart TV hacking. The feed pauses, and I wonder what she's doing.

If she phones her father now, I'm screwed.

He asked me to watch Kayla, but I don't think he imagined I'd hack into her TV.

It's illegal. It's a breach of her privacy. I shouldn't have done it. But my need to watch Kayla, my obsession with the curvy beauty, is so strong that I don't give a fuck.

My fingers tap the desk nervously. If she calls her father, I'll intercept the call and send it to his voicemail. That'll give me time to close out operations here and destroy the evidence.

But she doesn't call her father. Instead, she types in a new search: "IT security Sunset Coast."

Shit.

She's bypassing her father and sorting it out on her own. She must realize he'd insist on her coming straight home if he knew someone had hacked her TV.

IT security. It's what I specialize in. I'm the IT branch of Bronn's security firm, and we're at the top of the search.

Shit.

We also claim to provide twenty-four-hour assistance. She taps the number for Bronn's company. She's calling Sunset Security. I have to intercept the call.

6
KAYLA

My fingers are still shaking as I dial the first number that comes up. Sunset Security. I don't care who they are or what they cost. I need to get that hacker out of my TV.

A shudder goes through me remembering the stranger's voice trying to have a conversation with me as if it was the most normal thing in the world. Who knows how long he had been watching me?

Dad was right. The world is full of creeps and assholes.

I glance over at the TV. The rectangle screen stares blankly back at me. Even though I've unplugged it from the wall, I move into the kitchen. Just in case.

"Sunset Security."

The voice on the other end is deep and calming, and immediately I feel some of the anxiety slip away.

"Um, hello, I'm wondering if you can help." I'm not sure where to start, so I just blurt it out. "I think my TV's been hacked. Is that something you guys help with?"

I desperately hope they do, and I brace myself for an

onslaught of being told I'm being paranoid. But there was someone in my TV and they talked to me, I know it. I even heard a freakin' cat meow. I'm sure I didn't imagine that.

"I'm sorry that's happened. It's certainly something we can help you with."

Relief floods me. They don't think I'm crazy. They're not going to lecture me about online security.

I explain to the man what happened, and the more I talk to him, the more I relax. But there's something that's really bugging me.

"Do they know who I am? Could they start following me or something weird? Like stalking me or something?"

The man is silent for a moment, and I bite my bottom lip.

"No. It's usually a random person who lives in another city, possibly even another country. They're unlikely to know where you live."

The fact that it's a random weirdo is comforting. Kind of.

"How soon can you come?"

We arrange for the security man to visit tomorrow, and I hang up feeling slightly better than I did a few minutes ago.

Before going to bed, I cover the TV with a blanket just in case.

7
SETH

The next morning, I knock on Kayla's door, feeling like a giant ass. She pulls the door open, and her eyes widen in surprise when she sees me.

"You're the seagull guy," she exclaims.

"Kayla, isn't it?" As if I didn't know. "I work for Sunset Security."

I pretend to be as surprised as she is by the coincidence, all the while hoping my guilt doesn't show through.

"No way!" she says, her eyes sparkling.

I pull out my ID card, aware of how she might feel about a strange man coming into her home.

She squints at my photo, then opens the door wide and ushers me through.

"Come on in."

The hallway is narrow with a closed door on either side, which I'm guessing are the bedrooms. The living room is at the end of the hall. It contains a single couch and television with a blanket draped over it, which sends a rush of guilt through me.

The fabric on the couch is worn, and there're cracks in the paint of the walls. The place is rundown, a world away from the pictures I've seen of the house Kayla grew up in. But she doesn't seem to mind.

"You want a coffee?"

I nod, and Kayla goes through to the kitchen. As she gets the coffee, she tells me again what happened last night. I nod at all the right places, the guilt in the pit of my stomach making it churn.

I make a show of looking over the TV, and she winces when I turn it on and ducks back into the kitchen.

There's a single window in the living room that looks out over the bay, and a small table is pushed against it with two rickety wooden chairs. I set my laptop up here as Kayla puts the coffee on the table.

I take her through a password reset and get a system reboot going. I could have done this remotely. I don't need to be here at all, but I wasn't going to turn down a chance to get to know Kayla.

"Do you live around here?" she asks.

Kayla's sitting at the kitchen table, a mug of coffee clasped in her hand. Her long hair falls over her shoulders and catches the morning light streaming in the window. She looks like an angel sitting there like that.

I pull out the chair next to her. My fingers itch to run through her hair, and I tap them on the wooden tabletop before I do something stupid.

"I live further up the coast," I say vaguely. I don't know

if she's being polite or if she's genuinely interested. "But I like Temptation Bay. I come here sometimes."

It's not entirely false. I've been here exactly twice. Once to accidently run into Kayla feeding the seagulls and then today.

"Have you lived here long?"

I hate making small talk, but I don't want to scare her by asking the big questions, like, will you go out with me? What do your lips taste like? And can I touch your hair? Yeah, even in my head I sound creepy as fuck.

I run a hand through my hair, frustrated at my awkwardness. If I was someone like Bronn, I'd sweep in here, tell her she's mine, and drag her away to my cave.

But I'm not a caveman. I'm a computer geek with a bad leg, and even though I know Kayla's mine, even though I've never felt this attraction to a woman before, I don't know how the fuck to proceed.

"I moved here a few weeks ago." She tilts her head sideways, and a strand of hair falls over her eyes. My fingers tap harder.

"How did you know I wasn't a local?" she asks.

My gaze sweeps over her silky hair and soft skin, the designer t-shirt. Even her pink satin slippers with delicate bows are designer.

"You don't look like a local."

She looks down at herself, at the big designer logo splashed across her t-shirt, and laughs.

"Yeah. I guess I should try to blend in more."

I chuckle, and it feels good, laughing with this woman.

She leans an elbow on the table and looks out the

window, and it's all I can do not to lean forward and kiss her.

Instead, I check the system reboot on the TV and set a software update going.

"You need to be anywhere? Because this could take a few hours?"

She shrugs. "I work in the cafe downstairs, but Mira is covering for me today."

The fact she's telling me where she works means she's starting to trust me, which makes me feel like an even bigger asshole.

I swear to myself that even though I know the new password, I'm not hacking her TV again. When I get back to my place, I'm getting out of all of Kayla's devices.

I thought I was attracted to Kayla when I saw her photo, but in the flesh, it's more than that. She's smart and funny and beautiful. She's the kind of woman I could fall in love with.

"Do you want to get lunch with me?"

I blurt it out before I have a chance to change my mind. I hate putting myself out there, but for Kayla, I'll bury my awkwardness.

She looks surprised and then a fearful look crosses her face.

I hold my hands up in a friendly gesture. "There's a fish-and-chip shop in town. We could get takeout and eat it on the pier, save some for our seagull friends."

I'm hoping that sounds nonthreatening and public enough to not scare her away.

"Sure," she says, and I let out a breath I didn't know I was holding. "That would be nice."

I tap at my keyboard, pretending to do some diagnostics on the TV, but the truth is, I can't look at her right now in case she sees straight through me.

The perfect woman just agreed to go out with me. Now I just need to not fuck it up.

8

KAYLA

It's got to be fate. When I opened the door to find the hot seagull guy on my doorstep, I knew the universe was trying to tell me something.

Not only is Seth hot, but he's also smart and awkwardly sweet.

I've caught him looking at me intensely a few times in a way that makes my body heat up. But he's been nothing but respectful, keeping eye contact and making conversation even though I can see it's an effort for him.

I was beginning to think the attraction only went one way until he asked me out. Even then, I'm not sure if he means it as a date or as grabbing some food while he's on a job. I don't care. Any time I can spend in Seth's presence is good.

He's the first person I've met here who I feel totally relaxed around—relaxed and safe.

"You never told me how long you've been in Temptation Bay," Seth asks as we stroll along the pier.

My hands clasp the warm paper that my fish and chips are wrapped in, the greasy smell making my stomach rumble.

"About two weeks."

He nods thoughtfully, something he does a lot.

"What brought you here?" he asks.

Now that's a very good question. I was suffocating under my dad's overprotectiveness. I couldn't stand seeing my mother cry. I missed my sister even though I was so proud of her when she went back to college this semester.

"I needed a change of scene." I settle on that because it's the truth, just not all of the truth.

"I know what you mean."

We stop by a bench that faces the water. I notice the awkward way Seth eases into the seat. He walks with a slight limp, and he rubs his leg as he sits.

I want to ask him about it, but it feels rude.

"When I got back from the military, I felt lost," he tells me.

"You were in the military?"

I can't hide my surprise. I had him pegged for a computer geek. I give him an appraising look.

When I think about it, he is buff for a computer guy, with broad shoulders and a hard chest hiding under his t-shirt.

My eyes run over his muscular arms, and there's instant heat between my legs. I wonder what it would be like to have those arms wrapped around me, to be pinned down by them.

He turns to me, and I hope he can't read my thoughts.

"Special forces. They need all sorts of, ah, specialist skills."

Oh wow. He was some kind of elite force, probably hacking into systems or making fake passports.

"Oh, that sounds"—it's my turn to be awkward as I search around for the right word—"impressive."

He ducks his head. A modest hero.

"Nah, just a bunch of guys doing what had to be done."

Wow. He's as modest as he is hot. And that's making me hot.

"Thank you for your service."

I feel humbled. I've done nothing with my life, and here this man is serving our country and getting injured along the way.

Our thighs knock together on the seat, and he turns to look at me. Our faces are so close I can see the different shades of blue in his eyes.

"You're welcome."

Seth's eyes flick to my lips, and I know without a doubt that he wants to kiss me. And Lord, do I want him to kiss me.

My lips part and I lean into him. His mouth touches mine, tentatively at first and then firmer.

White heat courses through my body, and the twinge between my legs grows into a throbbing need as his tongue finds mine.

With one kiss, Seth's making my whole body come alive in a way that I've never felt before. Sure, I've kissed guys, but never like this. It's never felt this electric, this intense, this…right.

His hand slides into my hair, and I feel every nerve

ending stand on end as he cradles my head, pulling me toward him and deepening the kiss.

A salt breeze whips around us, whipping my hair into my face and tangling us together.

There's a loud caw, and something tugs at the wrapped food I'm clasping on my lap.

We break away, and I feel the loss of him like a cold wind on my body.

"Hey!"

Mr. Red is flapping above me. He ducks his head and pulls at the takeout wrapper.

"All right," I laugh. "Wait your turn."

Seth stands up and shoos the seagulls away, and Mr. Red divebombs his head, swerving away at the last moment.

He flaps his hands and we both laugh.

"Guess they're impatient for their lunch."

My lips tingle at the memory of the kiss, but the moment's gone.

We unwrap our lunch and eat it with our thighs pressed together and a comforting warmth radiating off Seth.

We talk about everything and nothing. I ask him about the military, and he asks me about my life. It seems paltry next to what he's done.

After lunch is finished, we hold hands all the way back to my apartment. I want to invite Seth in, but it's too forward.

I don't know if the kiss was just a kiss to him or something more. And I know I should get to know him more before I invite him in, but I know in the deepest parts of my body that he's safe and he's the man for me.

Instead, he pecks me on the cheek, and I watch him walk away, dragging his bad leg behind him.

9
SETH

I'm humming a tune a few hours later when I push open the door of my apartment. Felix rubs against my legs, then looks at me oddly, probably wondering why I'm so goddamn happy all of a sudden.

Feeling like sharing the love, I scoop him into my arms and swing around the room. Felix sets his ears back in alarm, and I loosen my grip so he can jump to the floor.

He gives me an admonishing look and retreats under one of my desks, where he sits on his paws with his fur puffed out, looking unimpressed.

"It's okay, buddy. I'm in a good mood is all."

I sink into an office chair and bring up everything I have on Kayla.

It doesn't take long to disconnect from her smart TV and her laptop.

I no longer feel good about watching her the way I have been. In fact, I feel like complete shit. Her father employed me to make sure she was safe, not spy on her.

I bring up the connection to her phone and am about to disconnect that, too, when I hear her talking.

The number tells me she's speaking to her friend Marnie who lives in Portland.

"How's the cafe going?" Marnie asks.

"It's gooood," Kayla responds.

It's a private conversation. I should cut my connection and leave them to it. But there's something in Kayla's tone that makes me pause.

Marnie catches it too, the way Kayla draws out the ooo's in good.

"Ohhhh!" she squeals excitedly. "You've met someone!"

My heart rate jumps up a notch, wondering how much she'll tell her friend about me. I shouldn't listen, but I'm too curious to hang up.

Kayla giggles. "Noooo."

"Oh, come on. Spill."

"It's just a guy who I've seen a few times. Nothing's happened yet."

So she's not telling her friend about the kiss. In fact, she sounds pretty casual about it all. Maybe the kiss didn't mean anything to her. Maybe she doesn't feel anything for me.

"Is he hot?"

"Marnie!" Kayla sounds exasperated, but there's a lightness to her voice at her friend's gentle ribbing.

"Tell me, tell me. Is he big, strong, and hard? That's what we always said we wanted in a man."

My breath catches. My hand goes to my damaged leg. It sticks out from the chair at an odd angle, reminding me that I'm not whole, and I'm not strong.

I hold my breath, waiting for Kayla to say something about how smart I am, how clever and funny, and that being strong isn't important.

But she doesn't.

Kayla laughs. "Hard, strong, and bold," she says it like it's some kind of chant.

"Hard, strong, and bold," they say together, and I get this must be some childhood thing they did probably as girls.

They both shriek with laughter, and that's the point at which I disconnect.

If that's what Kayla wants in a man, then that's not me. I'm damaged goods. What can I offer a woman like her?

10
KAYLA

It's been two days since I kissed Seth, and my lips still burn whenever I think about it.

My lips burn and my core throbs and I feel restless and irritable because despite sharing the best kiss of my life, Seth hasn't phoned or messaged me since.

I was sure there was a connection between us. My body aches for him, and not only that, but I also keep catching myself wanting to tell him things about my day, wanting to share things with him I think he'd find funny. Like when I accidently put chili sauce in the ketchup container because I was thinking about his hands tangling in my hair. And I only realized when a woman shrieked after taking a bite of her sauce-laden chips.

Yeah, I thought we had a connection, but I guess I was wrong.

It's late afternoon, and I pull the door shut to the cafe. In my hand is the bread bag, and I walk along the waterfront looking for Mr. Red and his hungry flock.

I spot them a little way along the pier, harassing a figure sitting on a bench.

My heart leaps into my chest and I stop completely still. It's him. it's Seth.

A hundred things happen in my body all at once. I'm nervous and excited, my stomach churning as my heart races and sweat breaks out on my brow. How can one man have such an effect on me?

I'm not sure if I should go to him or walk away. If he wanted to see me, he'd have contacted me by now. I don't want to look like the desperate one by chasing him.

But I don't want him to glide out of my life either.

I approach tentatively, not sure what I'll say to him, anxious at what his response might be.

But when he turns to look at me, his eyes blaze with intensity.

"Hi," I say.

"I couldn't stay away."

He looks pained, and there's a troubled look in his eyes. I sink onto the bench next to him.

"What do you mean?"

Seth fixes his gaze on me, and a hand comes up to scoop a strand of my hair. He folds it between his fingers before tucking it behind my ear.

"I told myself I'd stay away from you, Kayla, but I couldn't do it."

My stomach drops. He's not making sense.

"Why would you stay away from me?"

He looks at me for a long time like he's trying to commit my face to memory. It makes me uneasy. I've only just met Seth, but I already know I want him in my life.

"Because you deserve so much better. You deserve someone whole, someone strong."

I'm not sure what he's talking about, why he's decided what I do and don't deserve, and why he thinks he doesn't measure up.

Then it dawns on me what he must be talking about. "Do you mean your leg?"

He nods slowly.

"I'm not strong, Kayla. I'm damaged."

He's talking about his leg. The relief is so strong I bark out a laugh. He frowns at me, and I immediately straighten my face.

"Is that what you're worried about?" I put my hand on his good thigh, and he shudders at the touch, his eyes fluttering shut.

"I don't care about your leg, Seth."

My hand runs up his hard thigh.

"I'll show you how much I don't care," I whisper it in his ear, a delicious boldness coursing through me.

I feel such relief to know that's the only reason he stayed away that it's making me bold. And his vulnerability tugs at something deep in my gut. It makes me want to show him how much he means to me.

"Come to my apartment."

He takes a sharp intake of breath, and his eyes fly open.

"Kayla…" It comes out as a groan as my hand moves up his thigh. "Are you sure?"

I think of all the reasons why I shouldn't invite a man to my apartment. Because of what happened to my sister. Because I've only known Seth for less than a week.

Because we've never even been on a proper date. Because I'm a virgin.

But my gut is telling me this is the right thing to do, that I'm safe with Seth and he's the man I want to give myself to.

"Yes. I'm sure." I take his hand and pull him up from the park bench.

11
SETH

Kayla leads me to her apartment above the café, and the whole way there I keep her hand tucked into mine.

I tried to stay away from Kayla. I tried to keep away. But I couldn't.

I kept watching her through the CCTV cameras around town, catching snippets of her figure walking down a street or crossing the road. It wasn't enough.

I needed to see her. It's a need I can't explain that starts in my gut and winds through my body all the way to my heart.

I came with no expectations, just needing to see her. Now, my pulse races, my chest lifts. This is more than I could have hoped for, more than I deserve.

Kayla doesn't care about my disfigurement. She doesn't care about my damaged leg. Kayla feels the same connection that I do, the same pull. It's a heady feeling, and as we walk to her apartment, I keep her hand firmly tucked into mine.

There's heat radiating from her touch. I'm aware of her body moving as she walks next to me, her elbow brushing my side, her floral scent of expensive body wash. After watching Kayla through a grainy screen, her presence is so overwhelming that it's all I can do not to take her in my arms, cling to her, and never let her go.

As soon as we're inside Kayla's apartment, I spin her toward me. She gives a gasp of surprise, and I close my mouth over hers.

Her body relaxes against mine and I deepen the kiss, pulling her toward me, needing to feel all of her soft body pressed against mine.

My hand runs up her waist and slides behind her back, feeling every inch of her pliant, yielding curves, her softness making my blood heat and my cock hard.

"Let's go to the bedroom." Kayla gasps the words, her face flushed with heat. Knowing she's as turned on as I am sends a fresh wave of desire coursing through my body.

She opens one of the bedroom doors as we practically fall into the room, our bodies pressed together with urgency.

My hands tear at her clothing, and I remind myself to slow down, to pull back, to make sure this is still what she wants.

With all the restraint I can muster, I take a step away from her, giving her a chance to breathe. The look of need on her face tells me everything I need to know, but I have to be sure.

That's when I notice the laptop sitting open on her desk.

I flick it shut, and Kayla gives me a questioning look.

"You can't be too sure."

Because if I can hack into her laptop, someone else can, and no fucker is going to see what we're about to do.

Kayla suddenly looks nervous. The boldness from a moment ago when she invited me to her apartment is gone. She clasps her hands together, standing in the center of the room, suddenly awkward.

"You still want to do this?"

I check in with her. Because even though my dick is as hard as one of the pilings from the pier, I'll walk away if she's changed her mind.

"Yeah." It comes out as a nervous squeak, and she smiles. "I do, but just so you know, I don't usually invite men back to my room."

Her brow furrows, and she looks earnest as if she needs me to know she doesn't always do this. I look around at the pink duvet, the pile of clothes on the floor, and the empty coffee cup on the dresser.

"I can tell."

She giggles and I use the moment to slide my arm around her waist and gently push her down onto the bed.

"You can change your mind anytime you want, okay?"

It seems important that she knows that. Kayla needs to know that most men aren't the assholes that her sister came across, that she has a choice and I'll respect that.

Kayla nods, and as her neck tilts up, I nuzzle her behind the ear.

"But I really hope you don't change your mind."

She laughs and I silence her with a kiss. She tastes like chips and soda and smells like the sea. It's a heady mix that makes my body tremble with need for her.

My hand roves over her body, slowly this time. Lifting up the bottom of her t-shirt, I plant kisses on her soft belly.

Kayla squirms under me. "That tickles."

"Oh, yeah." I nuzzle her belly, letting my stubble scratch her skin, and she arches her back at the sensation. "Should I go lower?"

Kayla's giggles turn to gasps as I tug her leggings off and plant soft kisses on her thighs. Her delicate skin heats under my touch, the tiny hairs sticking up under my hot breath.

Her leggings drop to the floor, and I run my hand up her thick thighs and over the mound of her pussy. Her satin panties are soaked and the sight of the damp patch, the feel of her wetness under my fingers, and her unique musky scent make my cock ache.

"You're so fucking beautiful."

Kayla sits up on her elbow. "I've never done this before." She bites her lower lip, looking nervous again.

"Oh, sweetheart. You saved your cherry for me?"

She nods shyly. With her hair falling over her bare shoulders, she looks vulnerable. It makes me want to protect her, to keep her safe, to look after her.

"I'll take good care of you, Kayla." I don't just mean I'll make her first time good. I mean I'll take care of her for the rest of her fucking life.

12
KAYLA

Seth's hot breath on my thighs and the scrape of stubble against my sensitive skin send shivers sparking through my body. I lay back on the soft bed, feeling overwhelmed by these new sensations.

My head's buzzing. I can't take in what's happening. I can't believe I've been so bold to invite him back here. I don't know if I've done the right thing. Then his mouth closes over my pussy, and all thoughts flee my mind.

The feeling is so intense, so intimate. I have a moment of embarrassment that he's down there, in the most intimate part of my body. Then his tongue flicks out and licks my hard nub and the embarrassment dissolves.

My body is on fire, and it's coming from the very center of my core. Every lick, every kiss, every breath singes my skin and makes my pussy pulse with a delicious feeling.

I grab the bedspread in my fists, needing to anchor myself to something before I'm swept away.

"Seth!" I call his name as I grind my hips toward him. An intense pressure is building, and only he can release it.

Seth's finger slides into my opening and I buck my hips, calling his name, the sensation almost too much.

He rides with me, his finger sliding in and out of my channel as his tongue swirls around my center.

"It's too much!" I cry out as a wave of pleasure engulfs me. I'm swept away by the sensations flowing through my body, a tidal wave of release lifting me up and churning me over and over on the shore of my pleasure.

My orgasm shakes my body, coursing through me like a tsunami, overwhelming every sense as it washes through my body.

Seth presses his mouth to me until the tidal wave of feeling dissipates.

When I come back to dry land, my fists are bunched in the sheets and I'm shaking.

"I've never experienced anything like that before."

Sure, I've made myself come, but not like that. Never like that.

It was amazing and intense. And I want more.

Seth slides himself down the bed and stands up. A wave of disappointment washes over me. He must see the look in my eye because he chuckles.

"Don't worry. I'm not done with you yet."

I reach a hand out, wanting him to come to me, to give me more. Then I realize why he's gotten up.

"Your leg…"

He paces the room a few times like he's walking out a cramp. I feel terrible. While I was experiencing intense pleasure, his leg was hurting the entire time.

"It's fine," he says. "I just need to find the right position."

I slide down the bed until I'm sitting on the edge. It seems easier for him if he's standing up. "How about right here?" My thighs slide open, and I indicate the space between them.

Seth stares at the place between my open legs, and his eyes go dark with desire.

"Perfect."

My core is throbbing from the orgasm, and I'm aching to feel Seth inside me. With renewed urgency, I pull off his shirt and help him out of his jeans.

Then he nestles between my thighs. His cock, long and thick, runs over my entrance, and I shudder in anticipation.

I should tell him to put a condom on, but I don't have any and I don't want to ruin the moment and a part of me just doesn't want to. I'm already doing something I shouldn't today, so why not go the whole way?

Seth's hand maneuvers his cock into place, and I lean back on the bed, giving him all the access he needs.

Seth thinks he's damaged but there's nothing wrong with the man standing before me. He's everything I need, everything I could ever want.

His cock runs over my dripping entrance, and I shudder at the contact. My pussy aches for him to be inside me, and I ease forward on the bed until his tip slides into me.

"You ready for me sweetheart?"

I'm nervous and excited and so full of need.

"Yes," I whisper, squeezing my eyes shut as he slides into me.

The pressure is like nothing I've felt before. My pussy feels stretched and I don't know if I can take his full length.

"Look at me," Seth commands.

I open my eyes and Seth cups my chin. "You're beautiful, Kayla. The most beautiful woman I've ever seen. I want you to look at me as I claim you."

The awkwardness is gone, and Seth is all commanding in the bedroom. His authoritative tone makes me shudder with pleasure, and I feel my pussy slacken ever so slightly. It's all he needs to push in further.

I'm stretched again and I groan through the pain, my eyes squeezing shut again.

"You okay?" He pauses and my eyes flutter open.

"It hurts," I say through gritted teeth.

"You want me to stop?" He starts to slide his cock out, and I grip his arm, the loss of his dick seeming worse than this intense feeling of pleasure and pain.

"No, don't stop. Don't ever stop."

"Look at me, Kayla. Keep looking at me."

As he says it, his cock pushes all the way inside me. I force my eyes to stay open through the burn. Seth's breathing deepens, but his gaze never leaves mine.

Seth moves slowly, sliding out of me and easing back in. My pussy relaxes and the pressure eases to a soft pleasure until I'm moaning with every thrust.

Seth grips my ass as he slides me onto his cock.

His eyes leave mine and I follow his gaze, watching as his cock disappears in and out of my pussy. The sight makes him groan, and I gasp as his thrusts become harder, more forceful.

He pulls me toward him, and the friction of his body against my clit sends shock waves through my core.

It doesn't take long for my orgasm to build.

"Seth..." It comes out as a whine because I need a release. I need his release.

He senses it too, and he pulls me closer, his fingers digging into my hips. I wrap my hands around the muscles on his arm, clinging to him as he slams into me.

The orgasm hits me by surprise. I scream his name as the waves of pleasure sweep me away and leave me spinning.

Seth stiffens and grips me as he cries out. I feel hot come explode inside me, and I grip his arms until my fingers turn white.

It seems to last forever, this moment in time. Entwined and spinning together through the aftershocks of our pleasure.

Until finally I surface, gasping for air, my body tired and heavy.

We collapse together onto the bed. Seth wraps me in his strong arms, and it doesn't take long to slip into a deep sleep.

13
SETH

Kayla's father answers his phone on the first ring.

"Is she okay?" He's anxious at seeing my number outside of our scheduled calls.

I think about Kayla's soft body pressed against mine last night, the low mewling sound she made as I licked her, and the way she gripped my arms until her knuckles turned white.

"She's fine," I tell him.

He sighs down the end of the phone. "When I saw your number, I thought…"

I cut him off before he can go into whatever he worries about happening to her.

"She's more than fine. Kayla's doing well. She's living her life. I don't feel right tracking her anymore."

There's silence down the end of the line.

"You're giving up on the job?"

He sounds surprised and irritated, and I try to see it from his point of view. He's a father worried about his daughter. He wants to make sure she's safe, but this isn't the way to do it.

"It doesn't feel right to tail someone when they don't know about it. She's not doing anything dangerous. She's making good choices." At least I hope she is. "You brought her up well."

"Does Bronn know?"

I rub my hand over my temples. I haven't spoken to Bronn yet. He doesn't know what I've been up to with Kayla, but he didn't want to take the job anyway. I'm confident he'll back my decision to pull out.

"Not yet. But he'll agree with me. Trailing young women without their knowledge isn't what we do."

"Not even when that young woman is in danger?" He's getting angry now, and I have to appease him.

"I don't believe there is any threat to Kayla. She hardly goes out. She doesn't meet anyone." Except me, I silently add. I'm the stranger you're worried about. Only I'd never do anything without Kayla's consent. Although even as I think it, I know it's not true.

I hacked into her phone, her TV, her laptop. I'm the man her father warned her about.

"It's not about going out these days. She could be being groomed online."

He sounds desperate and upset and like a man fiercely trying to protect his daughter.

"She's not."

"How do you know?"

I want to give him reassurance without letting him know how far I've gone.

"When you came to my office, you saw the set up I

have," I say cautiously. It's why we held the initial meeting at my place. Bronn knew my expertise would be needed and my wall of computer screens is impressive.

"I've been able to monitor some of Kayla's online activities, and I haven't come across any signs of grooming."

I don't mention that at her age it's not grooming he should be worried about. Kayla's old enough to be on online dating apps, meeting men in all sorts of legal ways. But she's not.

"I'm not happy about this."

"I'm sorry. But I'm not longer comfortable doing this job."

There's silence on the other end of the line, but he doesn't let his anger spill over. Patrick is a good man, and he accepts what I'm saying.

"I just don't think your daughter needs that level or surveillance."

We hang up the call, and I'm left wondering what he'll do now.

I tried to reassure him that she doesn't need watching, but I have no idea if he'll employ someone else to do what I've been doing. I can only hope that he considers what I'm saying and leaves Kayla to live her own life.

But there's no telling what an overprotective father will do.

14

KAYLA

One week later...

The bacon crackles in the pan as I turn it over, the hot oil making it jump.

"Something smells good."

Seth pads into the kitchen, his hair ruffled from sleep. His arm slides around my waist, and I plant a quick kiss on his mouth before a loud pop from the pan draws my attention back to the bacon.

"Can you put the toast down? This is almost ready."

A few minutes later, we're sitting at the small table eating breakfast while watching the fishing boats come in for the day.

In the last week, Seth has stayed over every night. We've made love more times than I can count, each time more intense than the last.

We've settled into an easy routine. Seth helps me open the cafe in the mornings and then disappears to work for the day. He always comes back in the afternoon when I'm closing up, and we walk along the pier, feed the seagulls, then go back to my place.

Seth's never invited me to his place, and if I feel uneasy about that, I tell myself it's because it's easier to stay here, close to my work.

It's been the happiest week of my life.

Seth is so easy to talk to, he's smart and funny, and I don't think I'll ever get tired of the feel of his muscular arms around me.

"What led you to go into the army?" I ask between mouthfuls of breakfast.

Seth takes his time. I'm used to that by now. All of his answers are considered and thoughtful.

"I wanted to serve my country." He takes a sip of coffee, a smile forming on his lips. "And have an adventure."

"Did you always know it's what you wanted to do?"

"Yeah." He nods emphatically. "Ever since I was a boy, it's what I wanted."

I wonder what that's like, to have a calling. To know with certainty what you want to do.

I've never known. Dad's always pushed me to go to college because he never got that opportunity. But it's not what I want.

I want something better, something more noble.

"I think I'd like to serve."

Seth almost spits out his coffee. "You want to go into the military?"

"No." I laugh because he looks so shocked. "I mean, I want to help people."

He looks relieved.

"I'd like to be a nurse."

I blurt it out quickly because it's the first time I've ever said it out loud. I've thought about it for a long time, and when I vaguely mentioned it to my father, he started going on about medical school. But I don't want to be a doctor. I want to be more hands on, to make people comfortable and help them heal.

"That's a fine way to serve." His support makes my body slacken with relief.

"I'm not sure my dad would approve."

I can imagine Dad's face. He's worked hard to get where he is. He worked his way up from nothing, as he likes to tell us, to own a successful business. He's always had big plans for me and my sister, plans that involve high-paying professions. I could never tell him that I want to be a humble nurse.

Seth takes my hand in his. "I'm sure your father would be proud of you whatever you do. He loves you very much."

It's funny. He's talking as if he knows my dad. And yeah, I guess after the initial disappointment I know Dad would eventually support my decision.

Seth brings my hand to his lips and kisses the tender spot on my wrist. The gentleness of his breath sends a delightful shiver up my arm.

"You'll make an excellent nurse, Kayla."

His mouth moves up my arm, trailing kisses over my skin. His support means more to me than he knows, and I feel a surge of warmth, a surge of love for this man.

"How long have you got 'til the cafe opens?"

I glance at the wall clock.

"About ten minutes."

Seth pulls me out of the chair.

"We'd best hurry then."

He's already got his hands entangled in my shirt, pulling it off as he drags me to the bedroom.

"Slow down," I giggle as I bump into the wall while trying to get my t-shirt over my head.

We both laugh, and a moment later, the laughter turns to kissing and we fall onto the bed, tumbling together, our clothes getting tangled in our rush to get them off. Knowing we haven't got a lot of time makes the love-making urgent.

I'm always aware of Seth's leg injury, so I climb on top, straddling him as I run my hands over his hard chest.

I don't even bother taking my bra off, knowing how good my breasts look in the expensive black lace.

Seth runs his tip over my entrance, but I'm impatient to have him inside me.

Taking him by surprise, I sink myself onto his cock, loving the way I make him groan. We rock together, our bodies fitting together perfectly.

His hands are all over my body, clutching onto my curves, his fingers gripping my hips as I slide up and down his shaft, riding his cock.

It doesn't take long for the pressure to build and then we're coming together, crying out each other's names as we explode in shared ecstasy.

I feel whole with Seth. I feel safe and warm and in control of my own life.

With a stupid, happy smile on my face, I dress quickly and go downstairs to open the cafe.

15
KAYLA

It's later that evening when I'm eating gooey, cheesy pasta straight out of the pan. Mom would never have let me eat this way at home and it's still a novelty.

Seth's at home tonight. He said he had some work to do, so I'm enjoying a night in my sweatpants in front of the TV.

I'm still wary of that thing, but there've been no more strange voices since Seth installed the updates, or whatever the heck he did.

Even though we've spent every night together for the last week, even though my pussy is sore and needing a break, and even though I know time apart is healthy, I miss him like hell. I miss his sturdy presence in my apartment, his shy smile, and his strong arms.

There's a knock at the door, and I swing my legs off the couch as my heart leaps. I'm sure it's Seth who's changed his mind and come back for me. But it's not Seth. It's my dad who's on the doorstep.

"Hi, Daddy."

I give him a quick hug, hoping he doesn't sense my disappointment. He pats my back in a tentative way, and I know straight away something's wrong.

"What is it?" I clutch my throat, thinking of my sister. "Is it Jo?"

He shakes his head.

"Can I come in, sweet pea?"

It's the pet name he's called me by ever since I was a little girl bouncing on his knee.

"Of course."

Dad follows me into the living room, and I sit on the couch while he remains standing. He sighs deeply and runs a hand through his hair. Seeing my dad worried like this puts me on edge.

"What it is?"

His gaze finally finds mine, and it's a look tinged with worry and sympathy. He perches on the couch next to me and takes my hand.

"I don't know how to tell you this, sweet pea, but that man you're seeing isn't who you think he is."

It takes a moment for his words to process. Then what he's saying hits my brain.

My chest constricts and my stomach drops.

There are so many things in that statement. Like, how does Dad know I'm seeing someone? I haven't told my family about Seth yet. And how could Seth be anything but the sweet, caring, smart man that I know?

"How do you know I'm seeing someone?"

I pull my hand away from Dad's because I don't like the guilty look on his face.

"I was worried about you, Kayla."

He says it like that explains everything, but it explains nothing.

"So you did…what?"

The possibilities are too much to imagine. "Did you spy on me?"

Dad looks away. "Not spy, no. But I wanted to make sure you were safe."

"Tell me, Dad. What did you do?"

"I employed Seth to keep an eye on you."

It takes a moment for my brain to catch up. "Seth works for you?"

It's preposterous. He's an IT guy, not a spy.

"I don't believe you. You've never liked the idea of me moving away from home, and now you're trying to sabotage what I'm doing."

Dad puts his head in his hands. "I wish it wasn't true, sweet pea. I really do."

"It's not true. Seth's a good guy, Daddy. He's smart and funny, and he's got a good heart. I know he does."

And I love him, I want to add. Because it's the truth.

"If you don't believe me, then come with me. I want to show you something."

Dad looks pained and tired. So tired. It's been hard for him to process what happened to Jo. No wonder he's coming here and making wild accusations.

I suddenly feel sorry for Dad. He's feeling guilty about what happened to my sister like it was somehow his fault that he couldn't protect her. And now he's being overprotective with me, inventing stories to make me come home. Well, I'll humor him.

"Fine." I stand up. "Show me whatever it is you think you know about Seth because I can guarantee he's not what you think he is."

16

SETH

There's a job that came in today that I'm working on for Bronn. I'm finding the vulnerable areas of the grounds of an exclusive country club further up the coast. I've got their CCTV cameras up on my screen, looking for dead areas where the cameras don't see.

Felix is perched on my lap, and every so often, I give him a rub behind the ears, making him purr contently.

He was upset with me when I came home, and I don't blame him. I've been back to feed him every day, but he's not happy I've been spending every night at Kayla's.

"You need to get used to it, buddy."

Felix purrs louder and I know I'm forgiven.

The doorbell rings, and Felix stretches lazily.

"Sorry, buddy." I shuffle him off my lap and pull myself out of the chair.

When I open the door, Kayla's father is standing there, his substantial frame taking up most of the doorway.

It's been a week since I resigned from the job, and I

haven't heard anything from him. If he's come to beg me to keep surveillance on Kayla, then he's out of luck.

"Sorry, Patrick. I told you I'm off the job."

He shifts uncomfortably and doesn't look me in the eye.

"Tell me again how you managed to check up on Kayla."

It's an odd question to ask, and I wonder what he's getting at. Is he still worried about his little girl?

"Look, whatever I did, I'm not doing it anymore. She doesn't need watching."

There's movement behind him, and Patrick steps aside, letting me see there's someone behind him. Kayla pushes past, her eyes are blazing mad, and her mouth is set in an angry line.

"You were watching me?"

Disbelief and hurt are written all over her face. I glance at her father. His eyes are downcast. He's obviously the one who told her, which means he's still been watching her. There's no point in lying.

"It's not what you think."

Kayla looks past me and into the adjacent room, the one with the bank of screens. She pushes past me and into the house.

"Is this why I've never been to your place?" She stops in the middle of the control room, her eyes wide in disbelief. "Is this what you do, Seth? Spy on people?"

"No." I shake my head. "It's surveillance." Which sounds lame because they can be one and the same. "It's security. I work in IT security."

She glares at me. "What does that even mean?"

"It means I use my skills to keep people safe."

"And did you use those skills on me?"

She's angry and hurt and there's nothing I can say that will make this any better. I look to her father because he's the one that employed me to do it. But I can't remind her of that. And besides, I didn't have to take the job.

I don't get a chance to answer because realization dawns on her.

"It was you, wasn't it? In the TV?"

My stomach drops. She knows, and there's no denying it. I don't have to say anything because there's nothing I can say that will make what I did right.

Her father looks up sharply. "You hacked her TV?" He's as surprised as she is. "I never asked you to do that."

Which is true. I came up with that bit of handiwork all on my own, like the creepy computer geek that I am.

Kayla's gaze flicks from me to her father, her head spinning so fast she might get whiplash.

"You asked him to spy on me?"

Her anger is directed at her father now, but that doesn't make me feel any better.

"After what happened to your sister, sweet pea. There's a lot of creeps out there. I had to be sure you were safe. I employed Seth to keep an eye on you."

"Yeah, well, he turned out to be the biggest creep of all."

Kayla's voice cracks and tears spring to her eyes. Instinctively I move toward her wanting to comfort her. But she takes a step backwards.

"Stay away from me."

The words pierce me right through the heart. But I don't blame her. After what I've done, I deserve her wrath.

"I'm sorry, Kayla. But when your father showed me a picture of you, I knew you were meant for me."

"Do you have any idea how creepy that sounds?"

"Yeah, I do, but it's also true. You're funny, smart, caring, and I love you."

It's the first time I've said it to her although I've thought it all week. She barks in mock laughter. "You're a creep, Seth. You're a freak. You made me believe you're something that you're not."

She turns to go and then swings back around to face me.

"The seagulls. Was that even genuine?"

I'm the biggest shit that ever walked this earth. I can't even look her in the eye.

"I watched you on one of the town's CCTV cameras. That's how I knew you fed the seagulls."

When I look up, there're tears streaming down Kayla's face.

"I didn't know how to speak to you, Kayla. I'm not good with people. I didn't know how to talk to you."

She shakes her head. The hurt and betrayal in her eyes makes me wince.

"It may have started off all wrong, but once I met you, once I got to know you, I took all the feeds down. I swear. What we have is genuine. Don't throw that away."

"What we have is based on a lie. Stay away from me, Seth."

She storms out the door, and I go to follow her, but her father puts a hand up and I stop.

His gaze meets mine, but he doesn't look triumphant. In fact, he looks as miserable as I feel.

"I'm sorry, Seth," he says. "But she had to know."

I nod. He's right. I don't hold it against him. He's protecting his daughter from weirdos like me. That's what a father should do. And he's done a good job.

Kayla is now free of the creepy asshole that tried to make her fall in love with him.

17
KAYLA

My eyes sting, and my chest is hollow. I grab a crumpled tissue from a pile next to my pillow and press it to my eyes.

They're dry for the first time since I found out the truth about Seth last night, the truth about men. That they are all assholes. All of them. Even my dad had me spied on.

A shuddering sob wracks through my body, and I clench the tissue in my fist until it passes.

I want to dive under the duvet, but I can't take any more time off from the cafe. Mira is about to pop, and I don't want her worrying about me or the cafe when she should be thinking about her baby.

My legs feel heavy as I swing them over the side of the bed. I sit on the edge of the bed for a moment, trying to muster up the energy to get up.

I was so sure about Seth. I felt so safe with him. How could he have hacked into my phone and my TV?

I think about what he said.

It may have started off all wrong, but what we have is genuine. Don't throw that away.

Can a relationship really ever be genuine when it starts with deception?

I don't know.

All I know is that my heart feels like it's been ripped out of my body. And if Dad thinks I'm coming back home after what he did, he's mistaken.

I can't even trust my own father. He was the one who put Seth up to it, I remind myself. But maybe Daddy was only doing what he felt was right to protect me.

There's so much going around in my brain that I can't sit still any longer.

Heaving myself up off the bed, I head to the shower.

All I know is I need to get to the cafe. I need to work to keep distracted, to keep my mind off controlling men and the pain they cause.

18
SETH

It's been three days since Kayla stormed out of my life. I've tried to call her, but she won't answer. And after what I did, I don't want to force her. If she doesn't want to speak to me, I have to respect that decision.

Felix mewls at me, rubbing against my leg. I bend down and stroke him absentmindedly, but he swipes at my hand with his ears back.

"Not you too, buddy."

It seems everyone's against me. Felix gives a pitiful meow and saunters over to his cat bowl—his empty cat bowl.

"Sorry, buddy." I'm even letting the cat down now. But the last few days have been a miserable blur, and I honestly can't remember the last time I fed myself, let alone the cat.

Taking a can of tuna from the cupboard, I open it and fork the entire contents into his bowl.

Felix purrs happily as he eats, easily forgiving me.

"If only women were so easy to please," I mutter.

The phone rings, and Bronn's number comes up.

"We're going out for a drink."

"Nah, man…" I start to protest, but he cuts me off.

"It's a team thing. Everyone will be there. No excuses."

The last thing I feel like doing is going out for a work outing, even if the security firm is made up of all my best ex-Army mates.

But it's not doing me any good moping around the house.

"Fine. I'll be there."

A few hours later, I'm at the Sea Hopper bar, slumped on a bar stool and trying to act interested in the conversation. But it feels like something is missing.

Every time the door opens or someone walks past, I look up thinking it might be Kayla. It's a stupid thought. We never came here. We barely went anywhere apart from her apartment.

Lyle's talking about the new motorbike he got, but I can't get interested. Bikes have never been my thing. I'm a computer guy. I don't know shit about mechanics.

Bronn has his arm around Adrianna, who he's clearly besotted with, and she's the reason he's pulled us all together. Adrianna's sporting a large diamond on her ring finger, and he wanted to tell us their happy news.

I'm happy for him, I really am. But it's hard to watch a couple so much in love when your own heart is breaking.

Adrianna heads to the ladies' room, and Bronn watches her walk across the room. He can't take his eyes off her. The goofy smile on his face is so out of character I wonder if she's bewitched him.

Adrianna disappears through the door of the restroom and Bronn finally looks at me. The smile slides off his face.

"What's happening man?" Bronn takes the stool next to mine and fixes his intense gaze on me.

There's no point trying to hide it. Bronn knows me better than anyone.

"I did something stupid." I take a sip of cold beer, wondering where to begin.

"Was it because of a woman?" he asks.

I nod slowly.

"It's always because of a woman," he mutters. "That pretty young thing you did surveillance on?'

I look at him sharply, wondering if I'm that obvious. "How did you know?"

Bronn chuckles. "Man, I've known you a lot of years. I've never seen you react the way you did when you saw her photo."

He's right. I was gone from the moment I saw Kayla's image.

"I should have listened to you. We shouldn't have taken that job."

I fill Bronn in on what's happened and how stupid I've been, how I've destroyed any trust Kayla might have had in me. By the time I've finished talking, Adrianna is back, and she's heard most of the story too.

They're both looking at me, their eyes round with sympathy, confirming that I'm a big ass and there's no come back from this.

"I think it's kinda sweet," Adrianna says.

Bronn chuckles and gives her a pat on the bottom.

"Yeah, because you're a little twisted, brat." They share a private look that's way too intimate for me to witness.

I take another swig of beer, wondering if I'll ever have a relationship like theirs.

"Have you told her how you feel?" Adrianna asks.

Bronn rolls his eyes. "Here we go. My fiancé the matchmaker. Watch out, Seth. She'll have you proposing before you know it."

She gives him a playful punch on the arm, and they end up kissing. I look away because it's way too over the top for me, all this public display of affection.

But Adrianna has given me an idea.

When the sin is so big, the forgiving gesture has to be bigger. I've got to do something that will make Kayla understand how I feel about her, something that will be so overwhelming that it trumps the way that we got to meet.

I push the stool away from the table and stand up abruptly.

"Where you going?" Bronn asks.

"To get my woman back."

There's the sound of clapping and cheering as I head out the door, but I don't look back. It's time to show Kayla how big my feelings are for her. It's time for a grand gesture.

19
KAYLA

My hair smells like grease from the cafe, my uniform needs a wash, and my hands are cracked from scrubbing dishes. But I don't have the energy or the motivation to look after myself anymore.

It's been four days since I walked out of Seth's place. Four long days of feeling like my chest has been split open and my heart yanked out.

Now that I've gotten over the shock of it, the lies and the betrayal, I miss him like crazy. It feels like a piece of me has been sliced off and cast into the ocean. I'm adrift without him. My life doesn't make sense anymore.

I came to Temptation Bay to find myself, but all I found was loneliness.

When I was with Seth, I thought maybe I could follow my dreams and be a nurse. He even helped me download the application for college. But now that all seems stupid, like I should just go back home and do whatever Dad wants me to do.

PROTECTING HIS CURVY GIRL

The only reason I'm still here is because Mira is going into labor any day, and I don't want to let her down.

I turn the key to lock up the cafe, clutching a bag of breadcrumbs in my hand.

I haven't fed the seagulls for a few days, and I wonder if Mr. Red misses me or if he's found some other food source.

There's a gaggle of birds further along the waterfront, and I wonder if it's Mr. Red and his flock.

I set off along the waterfront, my eyes squinting in the sunlight. The sound of the waves crashing on the beach, a sound I used to find calming, only rubs away at my soul. I feel empty, like I'm going through the motions of living without really living.

As I get further along the waterfront, I notice the birds swarming around someone on a bench. They must have found an alternate food source. My heart jumps to life thinking it might be Seth.

I squint into the sun but can't see the loan figure on the park bench properly.

It won't be him, I tell myself. I told him he was a creep. I told him I never wanted to see him again. But now I'm not sure if that's true.

As I approach the bench, the figure turns, and I forget to breathe. It's Seth.

His hair is a shaggy mess, and there's a dark shadow where he hasn't shaved. But he still takes my breath away, despite everything.

I stop where I am, and we stare at each other for a moment.

"Did your cameras tell you I'd be here?"

He winces at my harsh tone, and I almost feel sorry for him. Almost, but not quite.

"No. I haven't watched you through a camera since that first night we spent together."

If I'm supposed to be comforted by that, I'm not.

"But you did watch me?"

He hangs his head, and I feel a bit bad for him, like I'm being too harsh. Afterall, it was my father who employed him.

Seth raises his head and looks me in the eye. I thought I'd see shame on his face, but instead he looks defiant.

"Kayla. I've been thinking a lot about what I did."

"Spying on me, you mean?"

He holds up a hand. "Let me finish and then you can judge me."

I put my hands on my hips. I've already judged him, but I'm willing to listen. I can't imagine what he could say that would make me trust him again, but God dammit, I want him to try.

"I don't regret anything."

My eyebrows shoot up my forehead. It's not the apology I was expecting.

"I don't regret taking the job because from the moment I saw your photo, you woke something in me. I've never felt like that before, Kayla. I was intrigued by you. I had to find out all about you. I had to know you. No woman has awakened that in me before. No one before you, Kayla. And when I saw you, that was it. I knew you'd be mine. You became my obsession."

His words make my skin prickle. He's so sincere, so

intense. It's hypnotizing, what he's saying. Because I know it's true.

"I don't regret hacking into your TV. It fed my obsession. It allowed me to observe you, to start to get to know you. It fed this obsession for you that was growing in my soul and eating me from the inside. I knew it had to stop. I tried turning the screens off. But you haunted my dreams. Your image, the softness of your skin, the way you laughed, your easy smile."

Seth stands up and continues speaking, his eyes never leaving mine. As he speaks, I find it harder and harder to breathe under his intensity, the yearning in my heart for him intensifying with every word.

"I don't regret engineering a meeting with you because I didn't know how else to talk to you, Kayla. I had to find out if my obsession was founded on anything more than your heart-stopping beauty. I had to get to know you, to find out if you were who my heart told me you were, who my heart knew you were from the moment I saw your picture. I had to know if you were my soul mate, the woman I want to spend the rest of my life with."

Seth slides down on one knee, his bad knee bent in a way that I know must hurt him, but he doesn't show any pain.

He pulls a ring out of his pocket and holds it out to me.

"My heart knew it since the moment I first saw you, but after getting to know you, my soul knows it too. I love you, Kayla, and I want to spend the rest of my life with you. Will you marry me?"

I'm so surprised that I forget to breathe. I try to take in

his words, his declaration of love that fills my heart and opens my chest.

All the pain from the last few days leaves my body, and I feel hope and warmth and love.

Seth's words are like a balm to my hurting soul. The obsession makes sense. And it makes me hot to know that this man was so obsessed he broke his own moral code, that he craved me so badly he did whatever it took to get into my life.

It's crazy. I know it's crazy, but the way we met, the things he did, don't seem so bad to me now.

Seth's looking at me with a hopeful look in his eyes. There's pain there too.

"Oh, shoot. Your leg."

I put my hand on his arm to pull him to his feet, but he shakes his head. "Not until you give me an answer."

The answer's easy. "Yes," I say. "Yes, you crazy man. I'll marry you."

Seth beams as he slips the ring onto my finger, and only then does he pull himself onto his feet. He grits his teeth, trying not to let me see, but I know how much trouble his injury gives him.

"I've missed you," I say.

He pulls me toward him and runs his strong hands up my back and buries them in my hair.

"I've missed you too."

As his lips meet mine, my heart feels full. The emptiness from the last few days is gone. I feel whole again. I feel safe.

I know that Seth did what he did to get close to me,

and that's the kind of love I want, the obsessive kind that grabs you by the soul and doesn't let you go.

I tip the last of my bread onto the ground, and as the seagulls fight over it, we kiss long and hard.

My heart is full. It may be an unconventional way to meet, but it's what we have, and I wouldn't have it any other way.

EPILOGUE

KAYLA

Six years later...

"Goodnight," I call to the night matron as I scan my card that releases the doors to the ward.

It's been another exhausting shift. Working in accident and emergency always is. But I saved a life today and helped many others to repair and heal. I'm exhausted but satisfied.

Sweeping my hair out of my eyes, I give a small smile to the camera in the hospital reception as I walk past.

Fluorescent lights flicker in the parking lot as I head to the staff parking area. My car's in the far corner directly under the CCTV, where Seth likes me to park.

I take my time getting in, letting my uniform ride up my thigh. My finger traces the edge of my skirt, making heat pool in my core.

The thought of Seth watching at home makes me tingle with desire despite the weariness of a long shift.

Ten minutes later, I pull up in our driveway. Seth

PROTECTING HIS CURVY GIRL

opens the front door before I reach it, which means he's been tracking my journey home.

That makes me feel safe, knowing he's watching, making sure I get home safe.

It's been six years since we met, and his obsession for me is just as strong.

I don't ask him to hide it. Once I got over the initial shock of how he'd watched me, I found the idea exciting.

I like knowing that Seth's keeping an eye on me. It makes me feel both safe and desired.

Seth presses his warm lips to mine as he slides an arm around my waist. There's a hunger to the kiss, which lets me know he was watching my little show in the parking lot.

My stomach rumbles, and Seth breaks away.

"You need something to eat."

He always puts my needs before his, my husband. Even though I can feel his hardness through his sweatpants, he knows it's been a long time since my last break, and I must be hungry. I'm thankful for his thoughtfulness every single day.

As we head to the kitchen, Felix winds himself around my legs, giving me a friendly greeting. I rub the old cat behind the ears and he purrs happily.

Seth puts my plate of dinner in the microwave to reheat as we chat about our day.

"Did they go down all right?"

When I'm on night shift, Seth does bedtime for our four and two-year-old. Not always an easy task, but he's a patient and gentle father.

"I had to read *The Gruffalo* five times, but other than that, they were fine."

My heart warms thinking about him reading to our children, passing on his thoughtfulness and quiet ways to them.

As we eat dinner, we catch up on the day, but Seth is distracted and can't keep his hands off me. I know he's been patient, letting me refuel before he takes what he needs from me.

His consideration makes me want him even more. I leave the pasta half eaten and give in to his touch.

"I missed you today," he whispers into my hair, pulling me toward him.

"Show me how much?"

As he leads me up to the bedroom, I almost trip on a toy rabbit, which lets out a wheezy squeak when I step on it.

The sound makes me giggle.

"Shh, you'll wake the kids."

We tiptoe upstairs like burglars in our own home.

I'm weary. It's been a long day. But I feel satisfied. I'm doing work that matters, that changes lives. I've got a loving husband to come home to and two amazing kids.

It's not the life my father might have wanted for me, but it's my life and I love it.

* * *

WHAT TO READ NEXT

HIS NIGHTLY OBSESSION

Mentioned in this book:
Read Mira and Sean's story in *His Nightly Obsession.*

I'm a simple fisherman with a dark secret...

Ever since I saw the curvy, troubled Mira, I knew she needed my protection.
I watch her at night, following her every move.
Her dreams become my dreams. Her burdens become my burdens to dispose of.
I'm a fisherman by day, her caretaker by night.
But she must never know what I've done to keep her safe, to protect what's mine...

His Nightly Obsession features an OTT obsessed male and the curvy girl he claims as his own.

Keep reading for an excerpt or get your copy from:
mybook.to/MSHisNightlyObsession

HIS NIGHTLY OBSESSION

PROLOGUE

Water laps softy against the prow of the dinghy as my oars dip beneath the surface.

Clouds cover the moon, making the ocean a black moving mass. But I know my way around the bay. I know how to row silently, avoiding the rocks and staying out of the beams from car headlights on the road.

I move quietly through the water, out of the marina and away from the jetty, leaving the lights of the township far behind.

Outside the shelter of the bay, the sea is choppy, and my heavy cargo rocks side to side in the bottom of the dinghy.

Putting all my strength into it, I row. I row until the lights of the mainland shrink to dots. I row until my shoulders ache. I row until the waves of the open ocean slosh over the side of the skiff, wetting my pants.

I row until we're over the place where the ocean floor drops off into the depths of the trench below. Only then do I secure the oars and roll my aching shoulders.

The lights of Temptation Bay are tiny specks, barely visible.

Mira is behind one of those lights.

I try to make out which is her apartment above the cafe, which light she's behind, and I wonder what she's doing now. Her soft, curvy body is probably lying in bed, her silken hair spread out on the pillow as she breathes softly. Asleep.

How I long to be lying next to her rather than out here in the cold, tending to business. I imagine sliding into bed next to Mira's warm body. The feel of her curves molding to my frame. The taste of her lips on my tongue.

But if Mira knew what I was out here doing, she wouldn't want anything to do with me.

I'm just a simple fisherman. That's what everyone in town believes I am. And that must be what Mira believes too.

My cargo is heavy, wrapped in sacking and tied with thick rope.

Crouching in the dinghy, I heave my cargo to the edge and push it over the side. The splash as it hits the water is drowned out by the waves. The package tilts on its end before quietly sinking below the dark surface.

There are boulders tied within that will help it sink, tugging it all the way down to the bottom of the trench.

Over time, the water will wear away at the sacking, and the fish will nibble at what's inside until there's nothing left.

With my business completed for the night, I pick up the oars and row for home.

GET YOUR FREE BOOK

Sign up to the Sadie King mailing list for a FREE book!

You'll be the first to hear about exclusive offers, bonus content and all the news from Sadie King.

To claim your free book visit:
www.authorsadieking.com/free

BOOKS BY SADIE KING

Series set on the Sunset Coast
Sunset Security
Men of the Sea
Underground Crows MC
The Thief's Lover

Series set in Maple Springs
Men of Maple Mountain
All the Single Dads
Candy's Café
Small Town Sisters

Series set in Kings County
Kings of Fire
King's Cops

For a full list of titles check out the Sadie King website
www.authorsadieking.com

ABOUT THE AUTHOR

Sadie King is a USA Today Best Selling Author of short instalove romance.
She lives in New Zealand with her ex-military husband and raucous young son.

Follow Sadie King on BookBub to get an alert whenever she has a new release, preorder, or discount!

www.bookbub.com/authors/sadie-king

www.authorsadieking.com

Printed in Great Britain
by Amazon